The Big Wave

Stefanella Ebhardt

Illustrated by Anna Crema

Play Station 1

1 Listen and match.

A

B

◯ Ermy is a fish.

◯ Pat is a boy.

2 Listen and write.

Ermy
friends
Pat

.... and .... are ....

3 Draw and write.

[ ] + [ ] = friends

.... and .... are ....

4 Listen and point.

A

B

C

D

5 Look at Exercise **4** and circle the correct word.

A beach / car / home / school
B beach / car / home / school
C beach / car / home / school
D beach / car / home / school

6 Listen and check.

Play Station 1

7 Look, listen and say.

8 Look at Exercise 7. Listen and match.

- ◯ blue
- ◯ green
- ◯ orange
- ◯ purple
- ◯ red
- ◯ yellow

9 Look at Exercise 7. Point and ask a friend.

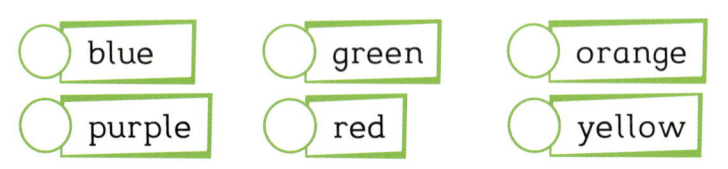

What colour is it?

It's purple.

10 Read and match.

- ◯ blue triangle
- ◯ green rectangle
- ◯ orange square
- ◯ purple circle
- ◯ red heart
- ◯ yellow star

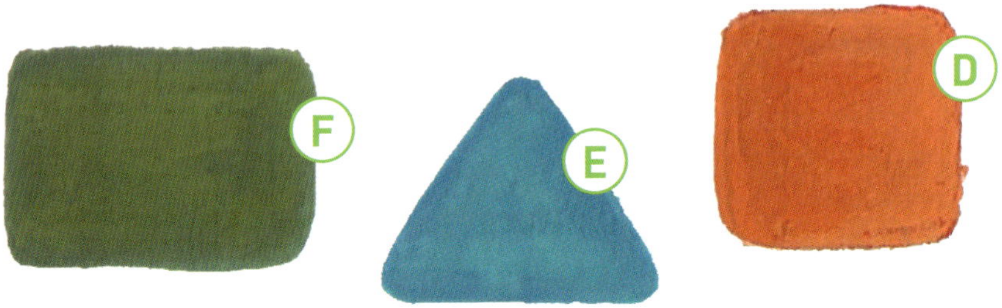

11 Listen and check.

12 Point and ask a friend.

What's this?

It's a heart.

Meet Pat and Ermy. Pat is a little boy
and Ermy is his fish.
Today Ermy is at school with Pat.
There are lots of children.
Lots of new friends for Ermy.
But Ermy's best friend is Pat.

What can you see?
Find:
• a board;
• a chair;
• a desk.

And Pat's best friend is Ermy.

Write.
My best friend is
....

There is no school today. It's Saturday.
Pat and Ermy are in the car.
Look, they can see the sea!
Ermy is happy. She likes the sea.

Put the sentence in order.
likes / Ermy / sea. / the

....

Pat is on the beach.
Look at Pat's sandcastle!
But where is Ermy?

Ermy is in the bucket.
'And the sea? Where's the sea?' says Ermy.
'I can't see the sea.'
She can hear the sea and she can smell the sea. But she can't see the sea.
'What's the smell?' says Ermy.
'Is it salt?'

Match.

A smell ☐
B hear ☐
C see ☐

Oh no! What’s this?
It’s a big wave!
Ermy and the bucket are on the big wave.
They are in the sea!

Help!
I can't see!
Where am I?

Ermy is in the sea. She can see now.
Look! There are lots of fish.

Wow!
This is great!

Point to:

- a big fish;
- a long fish;
- a round fish;
- a small fish.

And lots of colours. Red and blue,
yellow and pink, orange and green.
And lots of shapes, too.
They are big and small, long and short,
round and square. There are so many fish
in the sea! It's fun! Ermy is happy in the sea.

Ermy!
Where are you, Ermy?
It's time to go home.

But Pat is not in the sea.
He is on the beach.
He can't find Ermy.
The sea is very big and Ermy is very small.
It's evening. It's time to go home.
Pat is sad without Ermy.

Look and match.

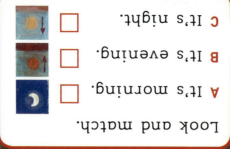

A It's morning. ☐

B It's evening. ☐

C It's night. ☐

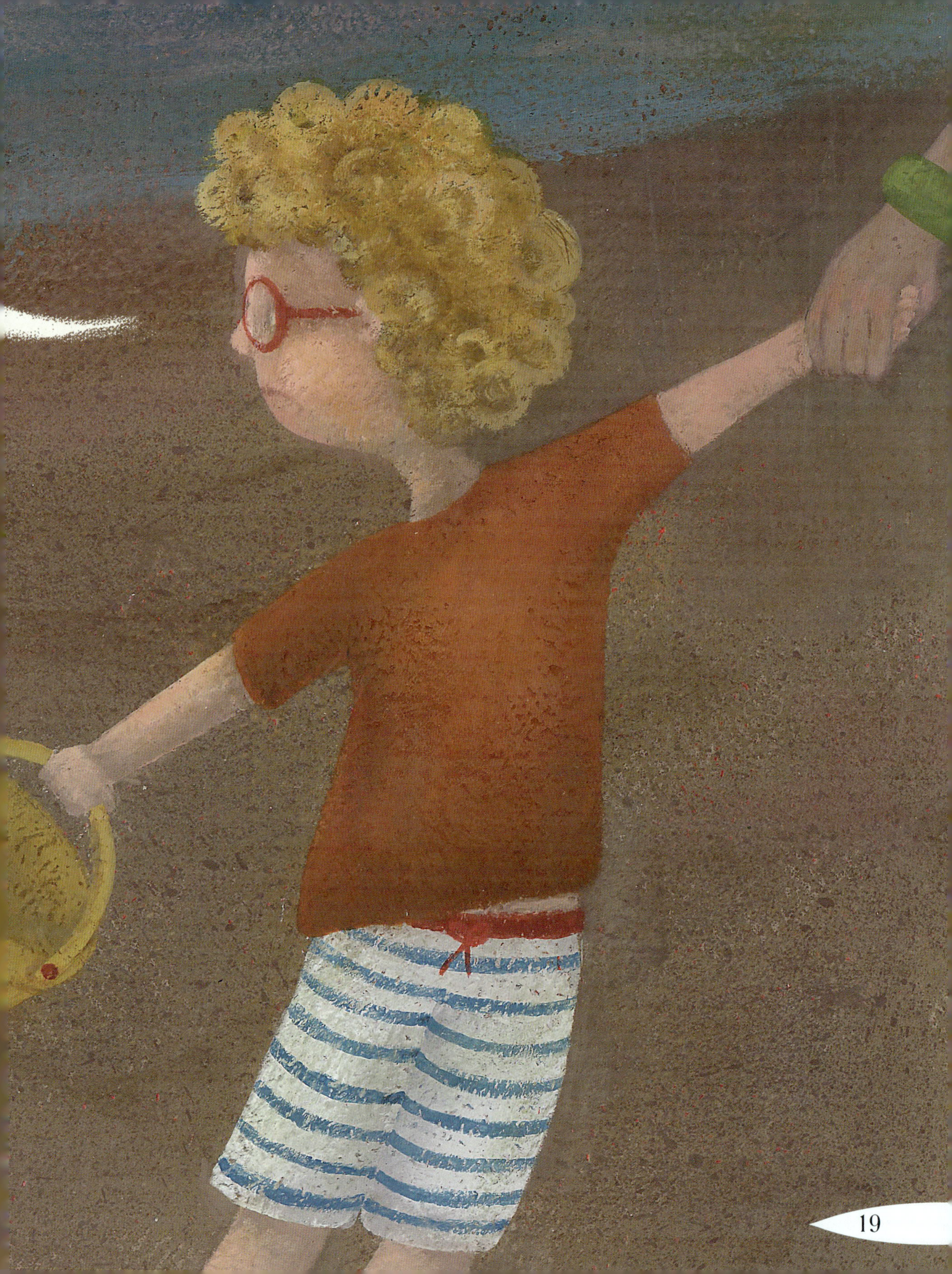

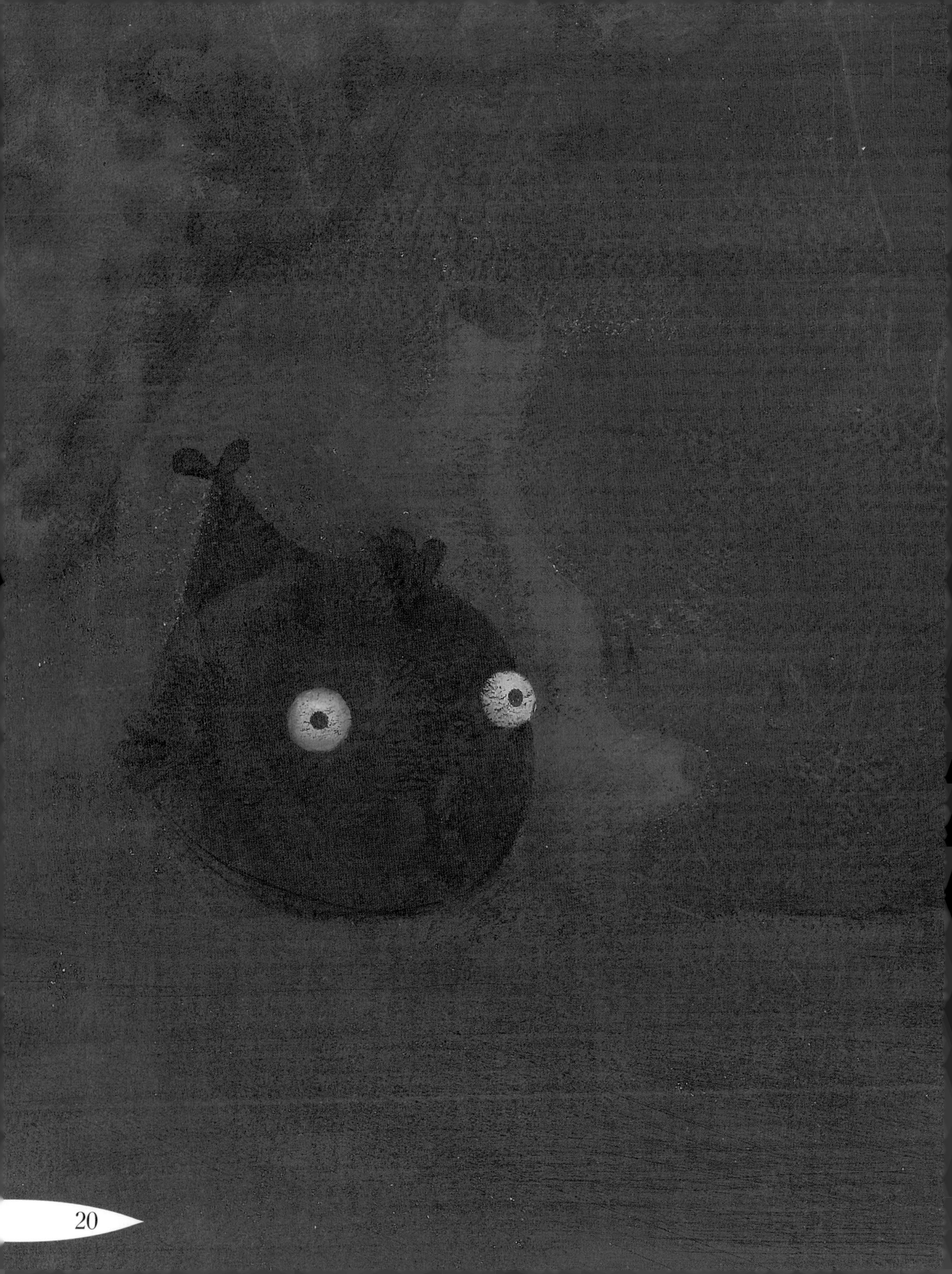

Ermy is sad, too. It's night and the sea is cold and dark. All the fish are in their fish homes. It's not fun anymore. Ermy is on her own in the big, big sea.
Pat! Where are you, Pat?
I'm scared on my own.

Oh look! What's that? It's the big wave again! Ermy is on the big wave again. The big wave can take Ermy back to the beach and back into the bucket. And back to Pat.

What colour is the bucket?
Tick (✔).

☐ orange ☐ red ☐ yellow

Ermy is back home again with Pat.
She is safe and happy.
Ermy likes the sea but she likes Pat more.

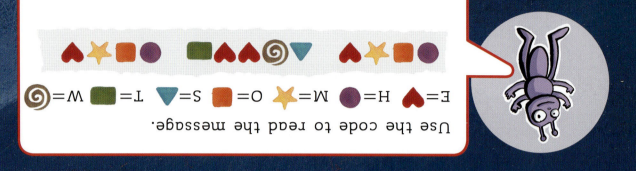

Use the code to read the message.

E= H= M= O= S= T= W=

____ _____ ____

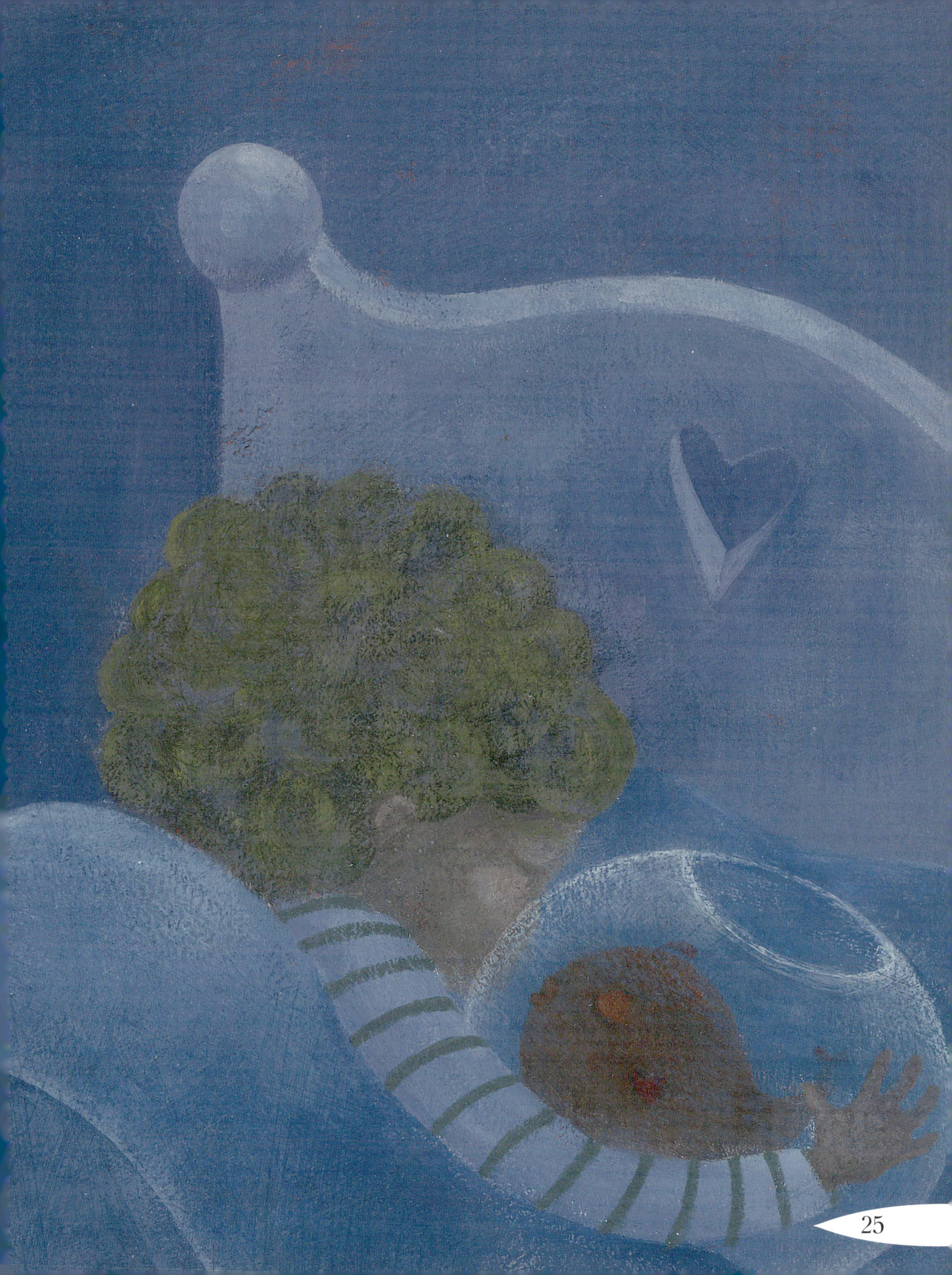

Play Station 2

1 Listen and point.

A

B

C

D

2 Look at Exercise 1. Read, listen and match.

- ◯ Ermy and the bucket are on the big wave.
- ◯ Ermy is happy in the sea.
- ◯ Ermy is on the big wave again.
- ◯ Ermy is sad in the sea.

3 **Read and circle the correct word.**

A Ermy is / isn't in the bucket.

B Pat is / isn't happy.

C Pat is / isn't sad.

D Ermy is / isn't in the bucket.

E Pat is / isn't happy.

F Pat is / isn't sad.

4 **Mime and ask a friend.**

Play Station 2

5 **Look, find and match.**

A beach
B bucket
C fish
D girl
E sandcastle
F sea
G wave

6 **Find and circle the words.**

p b o y c x b e a c h p f i s h w s e a e w a v e z b u c k e t r s a n d c a s t l e

7 **Read and colour.**

blue pink white

green yellow black

red purple

orange brown

8 **Listen and tick (✔).**

A

B

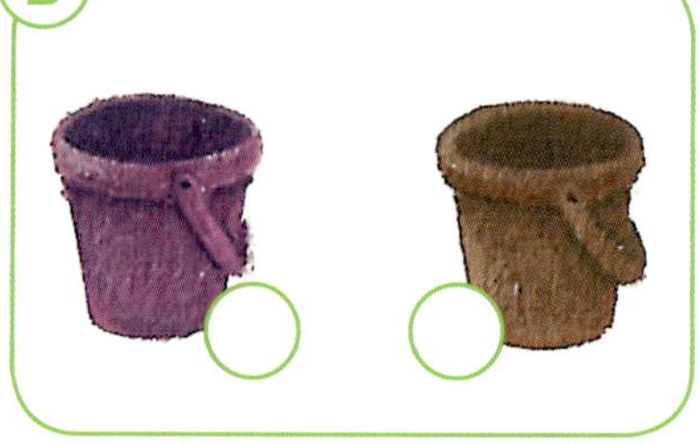

C

D

Play Station 2

9 **Look and match.**

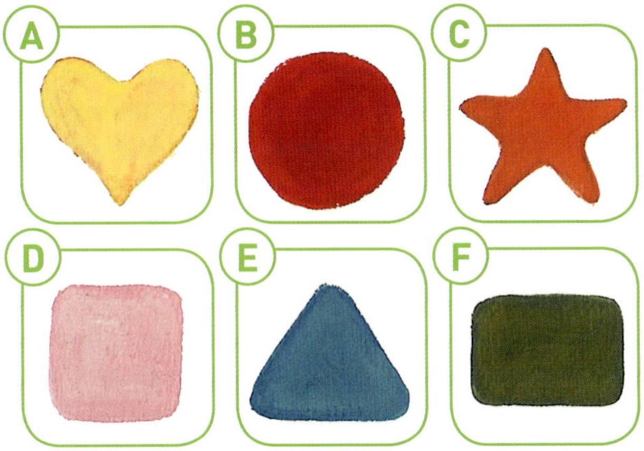

- ◯ A blue triangle.
- ◯ A green rectangle.
- ◯ A pink square.
- ◯ A red circle.
- ◯ An orange star.
- ◯ A yellow heart.

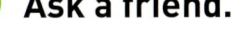

10 **Ask a friend.**

11 Listen and say the chant. Mime the shapes.

CHANT

In the sea, under the water, there's a triangle.

In the sea, under the water, there's a triangle
and a square.

In the sea, under the water, there's a triangle
and a square and a star.

In the sea, under the water, there's a triangle
and a square and a star and a circle.

In the sea, under the water, there's a triangle
and a square and a star and a circle and a rectangle.

In the sea, under the water, there's a triangle
and a square and a star and a circle and
a rectangle and a heart.

12 Read and listen to Exercise 11. Draw the sea picture.

Play Station Project

Shape pictures

Make pictures using shapes.

You need:

Paper or card

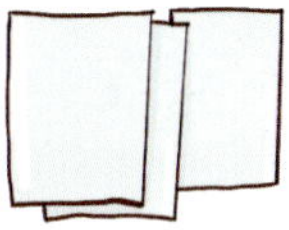

Colours

Scissors

Glue

1 Draw and colour different shapes on the paper.

2 Cut out the shapes with the scissors.

3 Arrange the shapes on another piece of paper to make a picture.

4 Now glue your shapes to complete your picture.

Go to www.helblingyoungreaders.com to download this page.